Mrs. Harrison

From his home on the other side of the moon, Father Time summoned eight of his most trusted storytellers to bring a message of hope to all children. Their mission was to spread magical tales throughout the world: tales that remind us that we all belong to one family, one world; that our hearts speak the same language, no matter where we live or how different we look or sound; and that we each have the right to be loved, to be nurtured, and to reach for a dream.

This is one of their stories.
Listen with your heart and share the magic.

FOR SYLVIE AND
HER UNCLE RICK,
WHOSE CAPACITY
TO LOVE HAS
AWAKENED OUR
HEARTS.

Our thanks to artists Shanna Grotenhuis, Jane Portaluppi, and Mindi Sarko,
as well as Sharon Beckett, Yoshie Brady, Andrea Cascardi, Solveig Chandler, Jun Deguchi,
Akiko Eguchi, Liz Gordon, Tetsuo Ishida, William Levy, Michael Lynton, Masaru Nakamura,
Steve Ouimet, Tomoko Sato, Isamu Senda, Minoru Shibuya, Jan Smith, and Hideaki Suda.

THE GIANT'S GARDEN

Inspired by Oscar Wilde's *The Selfish Giant*

Flavia Weedn & Lisa Weedn Gilbert

Illustrated by Flavia Weedn

HYPERION • New York

Once upon a time, behind the castle of a great Giant, there was the most beautiful garden in all the world. It was alive with every color of the rainbow. Tall fruit trees, fragrant flowers, and blossoming vines covered the land and provided a home for songbirds and their families. It was an enchanting garden filled with love and life, and in many ways it was a paradise.

Each day, on their way home from school, children from the neighboring countryside would stop and play in the Giant's garden. They loved running in the soft grass, gathering wildflowers, making wreaths for one another out of dandelions, and climbing the fruit trees. In the summer the children would gather the fruit, laughing and delighting in the gifts the garden gave them.

The children were happy in the Giant's garden, as they watched the birds in the trees and listened to them sing. They thought that the garden and all who lived within it were like a family of nature, and that because they loved it so much, they, too, were a part of this family.

Now the Giant himself was fairly happy, but he had heard of a faraway land where other giants gathered to share their wisdom. He thought that if he visited this place, he might learn how to be even happier. So the Giant left his castle. When he arrived in the faraway land, he discovered it was cold and barren, with no trees, no flowers, no birds, . . . and no children. The giants he met there boasted of their power and greed, and believed that selfish desires were the only source of true happiness. For them, life held no laughter, no joy, and no love. Soon the Giant forgot all about the beauty that life offers and the wonders of nature, and slowly he became just like the other selfish giants. He even forgot the sound of the children's laughter.

Finally the Giant returned home. And when he looked out his castle window and saw the children playing in his garden and heard their joyful laughter, his heart was struck with bitterness. He shouted, "GO AWAY! THIS IS MY GARDEN, NOT YOURS!" He ordered a wall built around the garden and had signs made that read: "KEEP OUT . . . NO TRESPASSING!"

The children were very sad and confused by this, and so frightened of the Giant that they ran to hide. They had done nothing to harm the garden—they had only played there, enjoyed its beauty, and taken loving care of it. They could not understand why they could no longer be a part of this beautiful place.

Time passed, and the children would wander around the high walls of the garden, remembering how happy they had once been. Then the spring came, and all over the countryside beautiful blossoms sprang up and songbirds fluttered in the air. But in the garden of the selfish Giant, it remained a frosty winter.

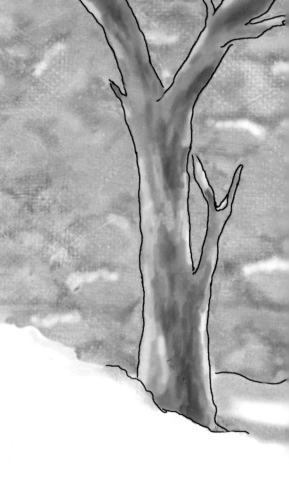

Within the garden the trees had forgotten to blossom and the birds no longer wanted to sing. The flowers had read the Giant's signs and were so sad for the children that they slipped back into the ground and went to sleep. Freezing snow covered the grass with her cloak, and frost painted the trees a shivering silver.

The north wind came, and then hail. Together they shook the roof of the castle and the trees in the garden with a frightening chill.

The garden was far from being the beautiful paradise that it once was. It was now sad and gloomy and so, too, was the Giant. Nothing that he had learned from the other giants in the faraway land was bringing him the happiness they promised.

Keeping the richness of his castle and garden to himself only made him feel isolated and alone. Instead of being happier, he was now lonelier than he had ever been. With sadness in his heart, he asked himself, "Of what use are all my riches without someone to share them with?"

Then one morning, when the Giant heard a
bird singing outside his window, a strange and
wonderful feeling came over him . . . as if his
own cloak of frost had been lifted from his
heart. The north wind stopped blowing, and
the Giant peered through his window and out
into the garden. He discovered that the
children, who also didn't want to be unhappy
any longer, had courageously crept through a
hole in the garden wall and were sitting on
the branches of the trees.

The trees were so happy to see the children again that they had covered themselves with blossoms, and the birds were singing on the branches. Flowers started to appear, and the grass grew lush and green right before the Giant's eyes. Spring had returned to the garden, and the Giant felt a rush of love inside his heart as he witnessed this beautiful sight. For the first time in a very long while, the Giant felt happy, and he realized how cold and truly selfish he had been.

Then he noticed that in one corner of the garden winter remained, and in this corner there stood a little boy. He was so small that he could not reach the branches in the tree above him, and he was crying.

Although the rest of the garden was coming alive again, this tree was still covered with frost and snow and the north wind still blew above it. The tree tried to bend its branches down to the little boy, but it was too tall and too frozen, and the boy was too tiny.

When the Giant saw this, his heart ached and he realized how sad he had made the children and how much he wanted their joy and laughter in his life. Deep inside he now understood that true happiness does not come from greed or selfishness—it comes from sharing the love in our hearts. And only by spreading kindness would happiness ever return to his life.

At this sudden awakening, the Giant rushed down from his castle to welcome the children back inside the garden. But when they saw him running toward them, the children ran away. As much as they loved the garden, they were still frightened of the Giant.

"Children, children, do not run. I have something to tell you," he said, trying to make them stay. But the children ran anyway. Only the little boy in the corner remained, for his eyes were so filled with tears that he did not see the Giant coming.

Slowly, the Giant came toward the boy, took him gently in his arms, and placed him on the branches of the tree. The little boy hugged the Giant, for he was not afraid of anyone who could be so kind and giving. Suddenly, the frost on the tree began to melt, the north wind grew silent, and the tree began to blossom.

The Giant called again to the children, "Please, please don't be afraid of me. My eyes and my heart have opened. I have changed, and I want to share this beautiful garden with all of you." And the Giant began to knock down the walls he had built around the garden.

The children had all been hiding, but when
they saw what the Giant had done, their fear
turned to joy. They came running back to the
garden . . . and with them came the full beauty
of spring.

"It's OUR garden now!" said the Giant to the
children. And together they danced and laughed
and rejoiced, as the birds sang and the flowers
bloomed in colors more brilliant than anyone
had ever seen before.

And so once again, each day on their way home from school, children from the neighboring countryside would stop and play in the Giant's garden. Only now the Giant would play among them. He would roll around on the soft grass with the children, talk to the birds, and delight in the flowers. They were like a family, and the Giant was a part of it. Feelings of love had replaced his cold and greedy ways. And just as spring had returned to the garden, it had also returned to his heart.

Never again would the Giant be selfish or unkind, for
he had learned a valuable lesson. And that is why, to this
day, behind the castle of a great Giant, the most
beautiful garden in all the world lives on. It is an
enchanting garden filled with love and life and the spirit
of giving. And to those who understand its beauty, it is
indeed a paradise.

Produced in cooperation with Dream Maker Studios AG.
Printed in Singapore.
For information address Hyperion Books for Children,
114 Fifth Avenue, New York, New York 10011.

FIRST EDITION
1 3 5 7 9 10 8 6 4 2

Library of Congress Cataloging-in-Publication Data

Weedn, Flavia
The giant's garden/Flavia Weedn & Lisa Weedn Gilbert;
illustrated by Flavia Weedn—1st ed.
p. cm.—(Flavia dream maker stories)
Based on: The selfish giant by Oscar Wilde.
Summary: A once friendly giant becomes bitter and builds a wall around his garden
where children used to play, but eventually he realizes how selfish he has been.
ISBN 0-7868-0121-2
[1. Fairy tales. 2. Giants—Fiction.] I. Gilbert, Lisa Weedn.
II. Wilde, Oscar, 1854–1900. Selfish giant. III. Title.
IV. Series: Weedn, Flavia. Flavia dream maker stories.
PZ8.W43Gi 1995
[Fic]—dc20 94–24498

The artwork for each picture is digitally mastered using acrylic on canvas.
This book is set in 17-point Bernhard Modern.